SANTA'S First All-Night Flight

ISBN 978-1-64349-297-1 (hardcover)
ISBN 978-1-64349-296-4 (digital)

Christian Faith Publishing, Inc.
832 Park Avenue
Meadville, PA 16335
www.christianfaithpublishing.com

Printed in the United States of America

SANTA'S
First All-Night Flight

Jeffrey Mason

As you know, Santa delivers Christmas gifts by reindeer and sleigh;

But did you know, it's not always been done the very same way.

There was a time long, long ago, when the number of people were few,

And he could carry the toys on his back to all the children that he knew.

But as the world grew, with more children and more land,

Santa knew he had to come up with a much better plan.

The elves had lots of ideas, and so did Mrs. Claus.

Someone said, "Use a polar bear, with his great big white paws."

Someone else said, "Let's use a sleigh pulled by a horse."

Santa knew he needed more, so he said no, of course.

Santa was looking out the window and happened to see

Some reindeer jumping and playing with so much energy.

So Santa watched them and thought, then later that day,

He said, "I know the solution! I'll use flying reindeer and a sleigh!

"By flying through the air, at Christmas magic speed,

"I can see all the children in just one night indeed."

So after some planning, and some very late nights,
Everything was getting ready for Santa's first all-night flight.

It was a wintery night in that land far away,
In a secret place that's still unknown today.
It's a wonderful city, a great place to be.
Full of fun, laughter, and joy, a real sight to see.
There are lights of all colors, that flash off and on,
And music fills the air with all Christmas songs.

It's a very busy place, everyone doing their chores,

Feeding the reindeer, making toys, and so much more.

There were some very, very busy elves;

They were wrapping, and packing, and pulling things from the shelves.

They loaded the sleigh full and looked at it with delight.

Now, they said, "We are ready for Santa's first all-night flight."

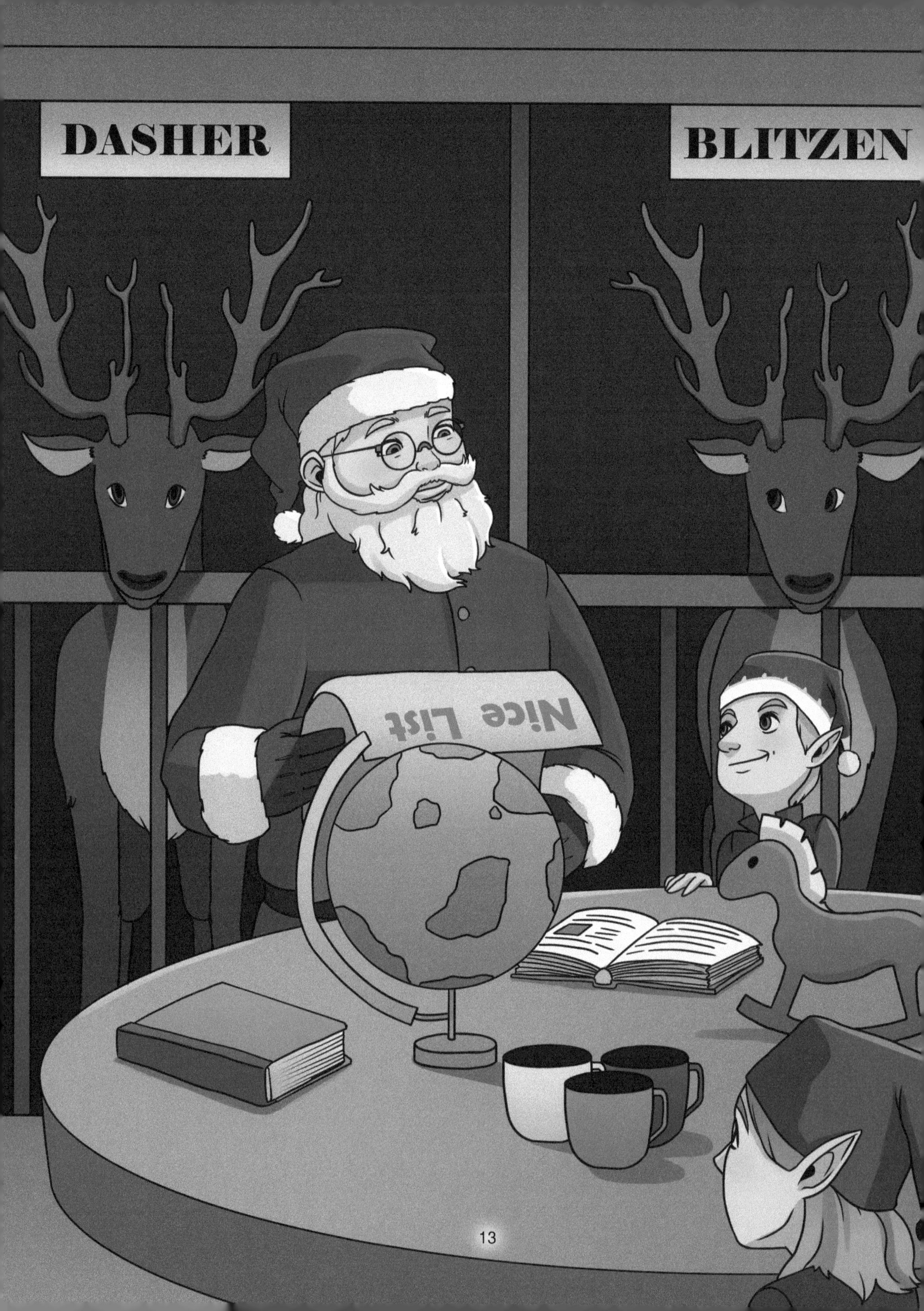
DASHER
BLITZEN
Nice List

Walking into the reindeer stables,

He came up to a big red round table.

He looked at his head elf, who was there to assist,

And he asked with a grin, "So where is my list?"

"All the names are written and I've checked it twice.

"And now I know who's been naughty and I know who's been nice.

"I have to be sure that I have all the right toys,

"To put under the trees for all the good girls and boys."

The elf handed him the list and didn't even pause,

Because the person who asked was, of course, Santa Claus.

He was dressed all in red, with some white furry trim,

And a beard that was white flowed down from his chin.

He asked, "Are the reindeer ready, all harnessed up tight?
"Everything must go smoothly on my first all-night flight.
"There are so many children in the world nowadays,
"But I know I can do it with my flying reindeer and sleigh."
Everything was ready, 'twas almost time to go
All around the world, to places with and without snow.
And then with a shout, up to the sky they all flew,
The reindeer and Santa and a sleigh full of toys too.

From house to house, from town to town,
Santa saw the rooftops, then he went down.
Delivering gifts to all good girls and boys,
Boxes with ribbons and bows, filled with all kinds of toys.

Some of the times, when leaving a home,

He glanced at a window, if any light was shown,

And as he looked, he was often surprised,

To see happy children with wide open eyes.

They'd wake up their parents, and run quickly down the stairs,

Seeing all the presents and stockings, excitement filled the air.

They opened their gifts; some were big and some small.

The children were happy, it didn't matter at all.

No matter how many, no matter the size,

Christmas was more than just presents, candy, cookies, and pies.

So what do you think, "What is the real reason
That we celebrate the Christmas season?"

Now, Santa's very first Christmas Eve with his reindeer and sleigh
Went so very well, that he continues to use them today.
And just like the first time that he flew into the night,
He is still keeping track of who's naughty and who's nice.
So even though you weren't there on that first Christmas Eve,
Remember that Santa wants us to always believe.

He errs who thinks Santa enters through the chimney.
Santa enters through the Heart.

—Charles W. Howard, 1937[1]

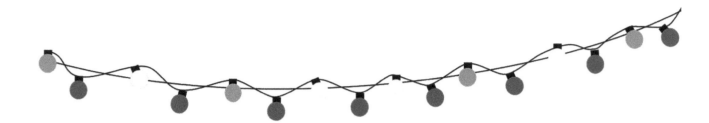

About the Author

Jeff Mason has loved Christmastime and everything with it for as long as he can remember. Every year in mid-October he begins decorating outside with many Christmas figures, such as a life-size nativity scene, a six-foot tall Santa, elves, and many others. Along with thousands of lights flashing in time to music for all to see and hear. Jeff believes in living every day of the year in such a way as to exemplify the Christmas spirit. He believes that the loving, sharing, caring, and smiling we see in each other during Christmas should be something we do all year long. He believes this is possible for all those who truly know the Reason for the Season.

He was born in Lancaster, Ohio, traveled the world in the U.S. Army, and now resides in Mobile, Alabama, where he plans to retire and spend more time on one of his hobbies, making toys for good girls and boys.

His favorite saying, taken from the movie *The Santa Clause*, is: "Seeing isn't believing; believing is seeing. Children don't have to see this place to know it's here, they just know." Jeff said that the best thing that could happen to him in this life would be to get a personal invitation from Santa himself to come and visit the North Pole.

CPSIA information can be obtained
at www.ICGtesting.com
Printed in the USA
LVHW070353140120
643553LV00006B/1053/P